Dear Parents:

Congratulations! Your child is taking the first steps on an exciting journey. The destination? Independent reading!

STEP INTO READING® will help your child get there. The program offers five steps to reading success. Each step includes fun stories and colorful art or photographs. In addition to original fiction and books with favorite characters, there are Step into Reading Non-Fiction Readers, Phonics Readers and Boxed Sets, Sticker Readers, and Comic Readers—a complete literacy program with something to interest every child.

Learning to Read, Step by Step!

Ready to Read   Preschool–Kindergarten
• big type and easy words • rhyme and rhythm • picture clues
For children who know the alphabet and are eager to begin reading.

Reading with Help   Preschool–Grade 1
• basic vocabulary • short sentences • simple stories
For children who recognize familiar words and sound out new words with help.

Reading on Your Own   Grades 1–3
• engaging characters • easy-to-follow plots • popular topics
For children who are ready to read on their own.

Reading Paragraphs   Grades 2–3
• challenging vocabulary • short paragraphs • exciting stories
For newly independent readers who read simple sentences with confidence.

Ready for Chapters   Grades 2–4
• chapters • longer paragraphs • full-color art
For children who want to take the plunge into chapter books but still like colorful pictures.

STEP INTO READING® is designed to give every child a successful reading experience. The grade levels are only guides; children will progress through the steps at their own speed, developing confidence in their reading.

Remember, a lifetime love of reading starts with a single step!

Step into Reading, Random House, and the Random House colophon are registered trademarks of Penguin Random House LLC.

Visit us on the Web!
StepIntoReading.com
rhcbooks.com

Educators and librarians, for a variety of teaching tools, visit us at
RHTeachersLibrarians.com

ISBN 978-0-525-57820-8 (trade) — ISBN 978-0-525-57821-5 (lib. bdg.)

Printed in the United States of America

10 9 8 7 6 5 4 3 2 1

ROBOT POWER!

by Celeste Sisler

illustrated by Dave Aikins

based on the teleplay "Robot Power!"
by Morgan von Ancken & Halcyon Person

Random House 🏠 New York

Buzz. Clink. Tap.
Blaze and AJ hear noises coming from Axle City Garage.

Gabby is making
a robot!

Blaze throws a ball.
Gabby codes
the robot
to chase it!
Beep! Boop! Bop!

Pickle and Crusher
see the little robot
zip by.

Crusher feels left out.
He wants to make
some robots!

Crusher builds
a chomping robot,
a throwing robot,
and a big blasting robot!

Oh, no!
Crusher's robots
smash through
a wall.

The robots
run wild in Axle City!
Blaze has
to stop them.

14

AJ and Gabby
design, build,
and code.
Blaze becomes
Robot Blaze!

The chomping robot
is hungry.
Blaze throws him
a metal bar.
Chomp! Chomp!

The chomping robot
bites the hard metal
and breaks up!

The throwing robot
is making a mess.
Robot Blaze
to the rescue!

Blaze tosses a log.
The throwing robot
trips over it—
and falls apart!

The blasting robot
is also making a mess.
Who will stop him?

Gabby and AJ have a plan.
They tell Robot Blaze
to use Blazing Speed!

Robot Blaze uses

Blazing Speed

to block the blaster!

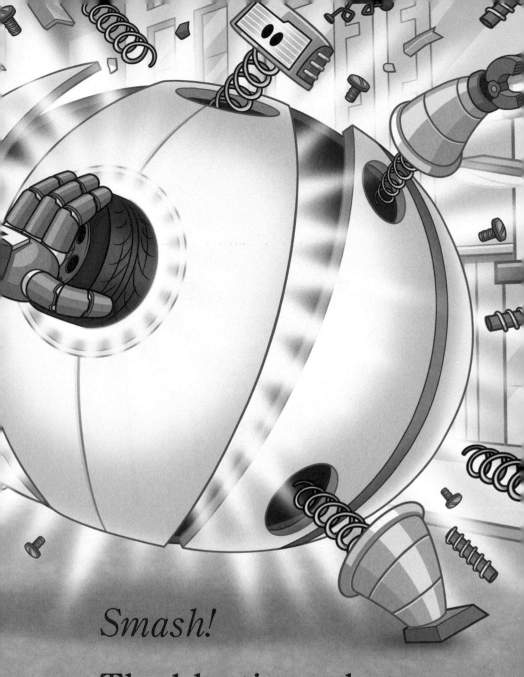

Smash!

The blasting robot
falls apart.

Robot Blaze saves the day!
His friends
cheer for him.
Hooray!